POPCORN

WITHDRAWN

FRANK ASCH

ALADDIN
New York   London   Toronto   Sydney   New Delhi

ALADDIN

An imprint of Simon & Schuster Children's Publishing Division

1230 Avenue of the Americas, New York, NY 10020

This Aladdin edition March 2015

Copyright © 1979 by Frank Asch

ALADDIN is a trademark of Simon & Schuster, Inc., and related logo
is a registered trademark of Simon & Schuster, Inc.

For information about special discounts for bulk purchases,
please contact Simon & Schuster Special Sales at 1-866-506-1949
or business@simonandschuster.com.

The Simon & Schuster Speakers Bureau can bring authors to your live event.
For more information or to book an event contact the
Simon & Schuster Speakers Bureau at 1-866-248-3049
or visit our website at www.simonspeakers.com.

Designed by Karina Granda

The text of this book was set in Olympian LT Std.

Manufactured in China 1214 SCP

The original Frank Asch illustrations for *Popcorn* are in the collection of the
Zimmerli Art Museum at Rutgers, The State University of New Jersey, New Brunswick, NJ.

2 4 6 8 10 9 7 5 3 1

Library of Congress Control Number 2014943085

ISBN 978-1-4424-6662-3 (hc)

ISBN 978-1-4424-6663-0 (pbk)

ISBN 978-1-4424-6664-7 (eBook)

To Mark Alan Stamaty

One fall night, Mama and Papa Bear
went to a Halloween party and left
Sam home alone . . .

so he called up his friends and
invited them to his house for his
own Halloween party.

While he waited for his friends
to arrive, he made himself a costume.

The first to arrive was Betty.
"I brought some popcorn for
the party," she said.

The second to arrive was Billy.

He brought popcorn too.

Bernie, Bonny, and Buster also
brought popcorn.

In fact, everyone brought popcorn!

The party was lots of fun.

When Betty said, "Hey, let's pop
all that popcorn," everyone thought
it was a good idea.

With some help from his friends,
Sam lifted Mama Bear's great big
kettle onto the kitchen stove and
poured in all the popcorn.

He added some oil and salt and turned on the stove.

Soon it began to pop.

POP! POP! POP!

There was so much popcorn, it quickly filled the kettle and spilled out onto the floor.

There was so much popcorn,

it filled the whole kitchen.

It spilled out into the living room.

It filled all the rooms downstairs
and crept upstairs.

There was
so much popcorn,
it filled the
whole house.

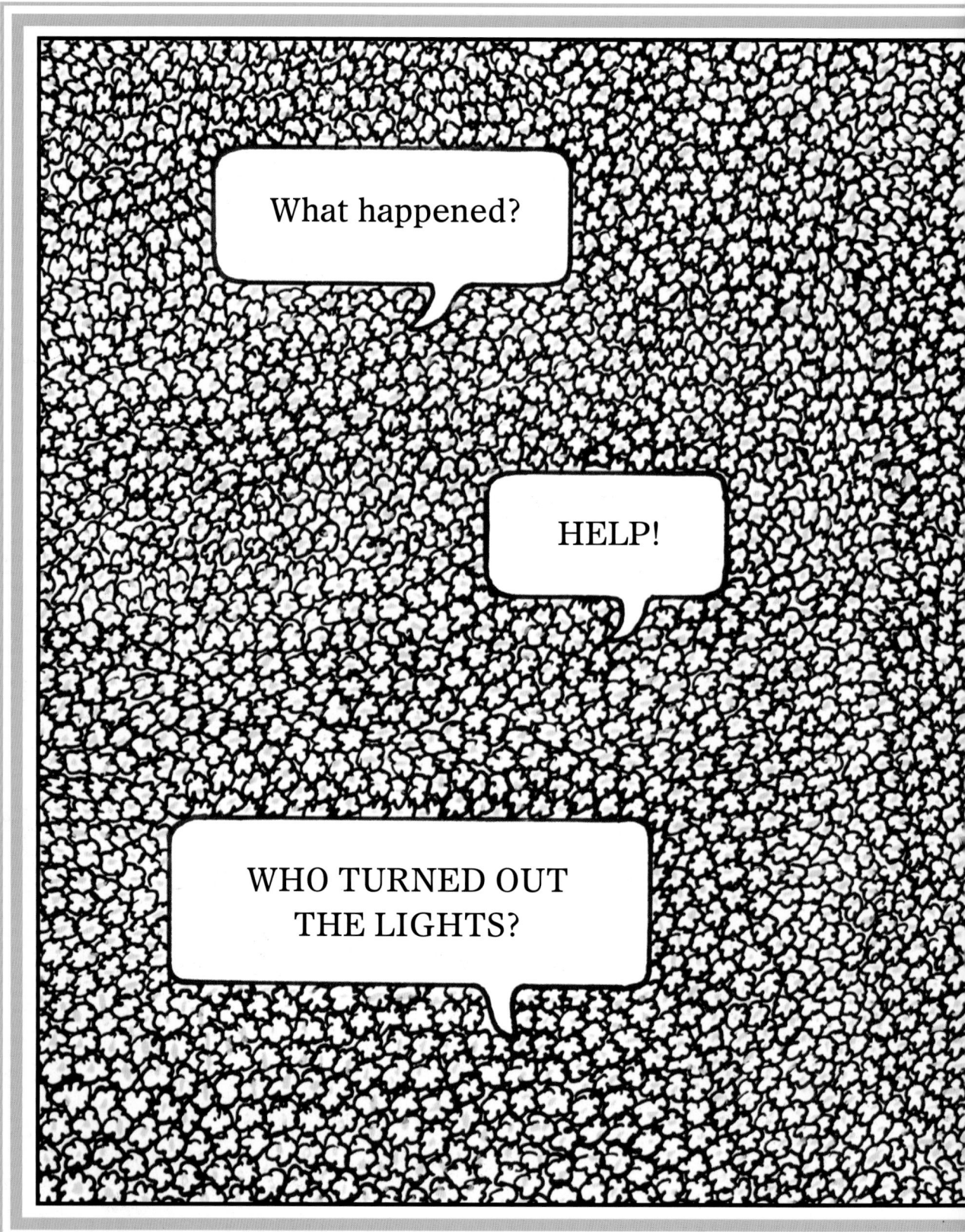

Everybody wanted to go home,
but Sam said, "No, you've got to
stay and help me get rid of all this
popcorn, or I'll be in big trouble."

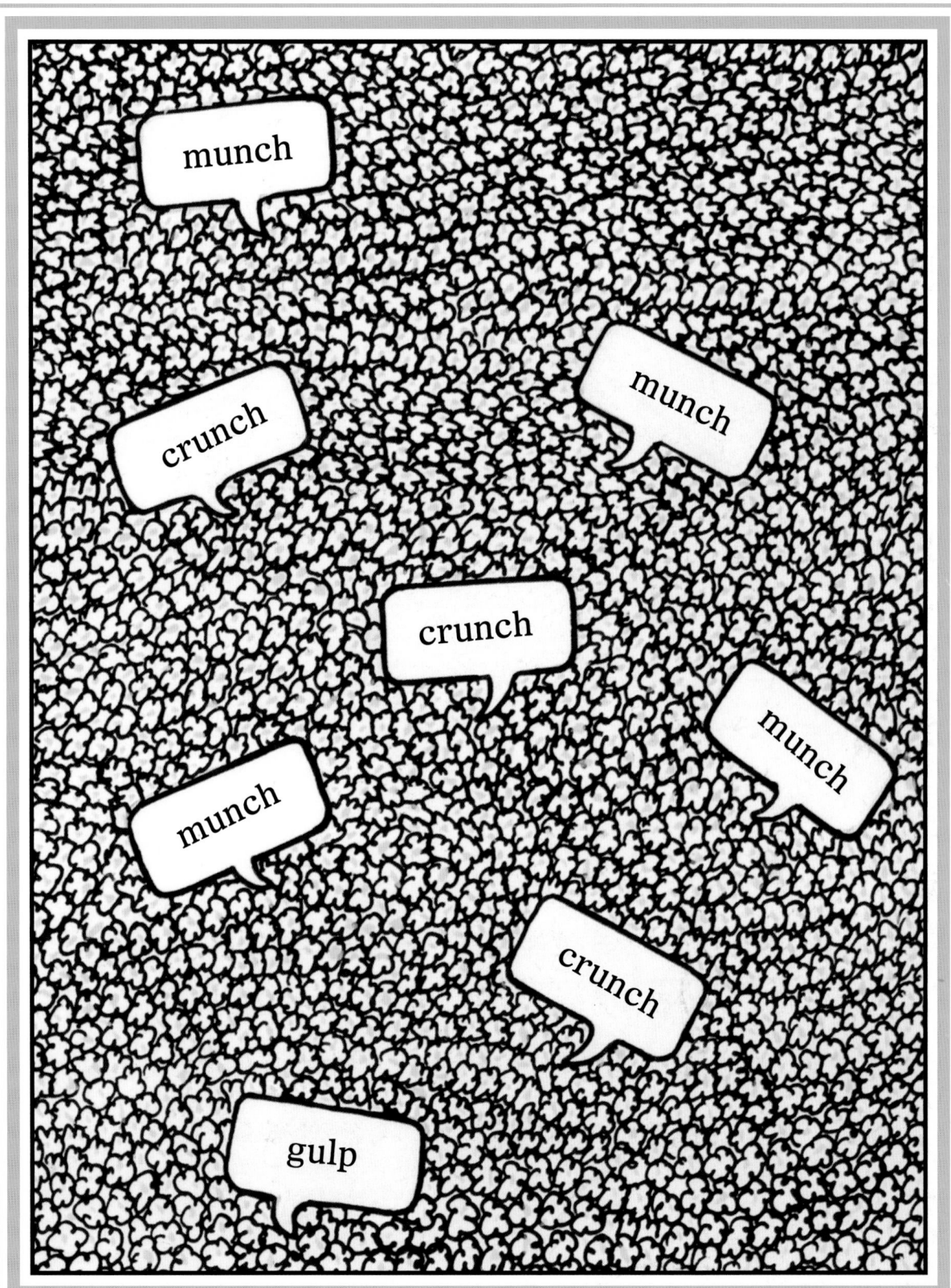

They ate and ate and ate . . .

and ate and ate and ate . . .

and ate and ate and ate . . .

until all the popcorn was gone.

"I don't care if I ever see another piece of popcorn in my whole life," said Buster.

"I feel like my stomach is going to burst," said Betty.

"Mine too," said Bobby.

Sam felt the sickest of all.

He said good night to his friends and cleaned up . . .

and went to bed.

Later that night, Mama and Papa
Bear came home.

"Wake up," they said. "We brought
you a present."